T0103645

Young
Lover

Kathy Hart

Order this book online at www.trafford.com
or email orders@trafford.com

Most Trafford titles are also available at major online book retailers.

Print information available on the last page.

ISBN: 978-1-4907-5580-9 (sc)
ISBN: 978-1-4907-5582-3 (hc)
ISBN: 978-1-4907-5581-6 (e)

Library of Congress Control Number: 2015902702

Trafford rev. 02/18/2015

Trafford
PUBLISHING® www.trafford.com
North America & international
toll-free: 1 888 232 4444 (USA & Canada)
fax: 812 355 4082

When people reach their middle age life, they might want to have that kind of wild sex sometimes, and if they can't get it from home, they usually will look for a younger person. But they have to remember that there are consequences that come with that. Age is only one. Of course, it can be fun and adventurous, but when things happen and you let your feelings get involved, it can also be heartbreaking, painful, and dangerous.

Chapter One

Sitting at an auto shop, getting her car fixed, Kayla stares at all the hot sweaty men while they work. Kayla's forty years old but looks much younger than what she really is. She has the body of a young girl in her twenties. She keeps her hair in styles that young girls wear. In Kayla's early years, she weighed over four hundred pounds. Now she's two hundred seventy pounds and working her way down, so her confidence and esteem have tremendously risen. Kayla decided to test herself. She walks around to see if any of them would notice her, and they do. While Kayla walks around pretending to look at equipment and liquids, she notices that the guy who's actually working on her car keeps staring at her when she's not looking at her car. Kayla walks over there to strike up a conversation. He tries not to look at her as she walks toward him.

Kayla: Hi. How are you?
Him: Hi. I'm good, but I'll be better once I get off.

They both laughed.

Kayla: My name is Kayla, and you are?
Him: My name is Garrett, but they call me G.
Kayla: Nice to meet you. How much longer do you think you'll be working on her?

G: I'm just about finished.

As they continued their conversation, Kayla finds out that G's only twenty-six. That's a fourteen-year difference. There was no way Kayla could see herself with a boy that young. They asked about each other's relationship or if they even had one.

G: Well, are you seeing someone at this time?

Kayla: I am involved with someone, but it's not really working out.

G: I and my girl just broke up, so now I'm living the single life.

Kayla: What happened?

G: I really don't want to talk about it.

What Kayla didn't know was that's what most people say when they're really lying. They exchanged numbers and went about their business.

One night, not too long after they met, G called Kayla and asked her if she wanted to visit him. Kayla agreed and started getting ready. G called back and asked her if she could bring him some liquor, beer, and cigarettes, and she agreed to that also. She met him on Beaver Street, where he stayed with some of the guys that he worked with. When she arrived, he came out to the car, where they talked and laughed for hours. At that time, they determined what kind of relationship they were going to have: no commitment and feelings involved and no strings attached. He made it perfectly clear that he was single, and that's the life he was living, which means he will be dating and having sex with other girls. No feelings will be created at all. After that, they said their good-byes and ended with a long French kiss. Kayla thought to herself, *Oh my god, this nigga got big lips, and he knows how to use them for kissing.* And those sexy bedroom eyes will make you have sex without him even asking you to do it. This made Kayla hot and horny. When their lips parted, Kayla glanced in the back of her car and quickly returned her eyes on him. He sat there smiling because he knew what she was thinking. He was waiting for her to make the first move, but she didn't budge. She wanted it to be right the first time. Kayla told him that she will talk to him later, and G told her to call him and let him know that she made it home. They said good night, and Kayla left after G went in the house. After that, Kayla never called him, and he never called her.

Six months passed, and it's spring. As Kayla sat at her computer, drinking coffee, she received a text message on her cell phone from G that says, "Tell your sister, Bri, to call me."

Kayla responded, "You have the wrong person. I don't have a sister named Bri."

G asks, "Who is this?"

Kayla replies, "Kayla with the red Tahoe."

All of a sudden, her phone rings. It's G.

Kayla: Hello.
G: What's good witcha?
Kayla: Nothing, chillaxin'. What's up withca?
G: A car but no gas.
Kayla: Same here. No car but gas.

Kayla's truck was down during that time. They made plans to meet that night. He picked her up from a restaurant, and she gave him some money for gas, but she was going to make sure that he rode that gas out driving her around. Riding around with nowhere specific to go, they stopped at the store for drinks and went to a motel room. As they sat there, drinking Sveko and cranberry juice, Kayla's hormones started jumping. Kayla's phone rang, and it's one of her cousins. While she's on the phone, G starts biting on her tits and kissing on her neck and lips. Kayla was so ready to fuck, but she asked him to stop, and he did. They started talking about a cabaret that one of G's brothers was having, and he asked Kayla if she wanted to go. She said yes and got on the phone to invite more people. At that point, he started rubbing her tits and kissing her again. Kayla decided this time she was getting off the phone and return the actions being taken. G stood up and took Kayla's cup out of her hand, laid her back, and pulled her pants off.

Kayla: Did you bring a condom?
G: No, I'll pull out. Just relax and enjoy.

As he indulged in the taste of her pussy, Kayla lay there moaning loudly as she enjoyed the feeling that was going through her body, gripping on the sheets, hitting the headboard of the bed with her hands, and fighting to keep her legs closed as he kept them open, making him even more hungry and thirsty for her satisfaction. Making sure she had multiple orgasms, he came up and lay on her face-to-face to kiss her. He notices tears running down her face.

G, looking confused: Why are you crying?
Kayla: I haven't felt this way in a long time.

G wiped the tears away and gave her a tender kiss. Kayla rolled over on him, slid down, pulled his dick out, and started sucking it like it was the last time. G lay there, moaning and rubbing his nipple and Kayla's head. Enjoying every bit of pleasure he was getting, he was about to cum. Just then, Kayla stopped and, without thinking about protection from anything, proceeded to climb on his rock-hard dick. Riding his dick as if she was in a horse race, she moaned. G grabbed her ass while he moaned and sucked on her tits. In a blink of an eye, G rolled her over and began to plunge his dick into her pussy. Kayla wrapped her legs around him, thinking it would ease the pain. Scratching his back with every plunge, he moaned louder and eased up.

G: You like it?
Kayla, with a soft voice: Yes.
G: Tell me you like it.
Kayla: I like it.
G: You want me to hit it from the back, don't you?

Kayla: Yes.

G: Then turn that ass over.

    Kayla got on her hands and knees. G went and started eating her pussy from the back. Kayla, going crazy, pulled the sheets from the end of the bed while moaning and moving around. G held a tight grip on her to keep her from moving far away from him. He then came out of the pussy and started kissing her ass and stuck his dick into her pussy softly. Going faster and faster, he started telling her that her pussy is good and wet. Kayla then started bouncing her ass up and down. G hit her on the ass continuously with his hand, making her bounce even faster and harder. Both of them started moaning to their satisfaction. Getting louder and louder, reaching their climax, their movement slowed down. The feeling wouldn't let them pull away from each other, but as soon as it was over, Kayla remembered that she was very fertile.

Chapter Two

T hat following week, it was time for the cabaret that G's brother was having. Kayla had bought everyone's VIP ticket in advance at regular. When they got close to the party, she called G to let him know they were about to pull up. When they finally arrived, he was standing outside waiting. When Kayla saw him, that sexual feeling came back again. As she approached him, they gave each other a kiss and hug. Kayla introduced him to everyone. They went in and gave their tickets to the ticket taker and started going to their table. G grabbed Kayla's hand and took her to his friends and introduced her then walked her to the table that her friends chose and gave her a kiss. Kayla felt special. Her nephew looked surprised because he didn't know she was dating a younger man, and when he found out that he was only a few years older than him, he was shocked.

Sitting at the table after being there for a while, Kayla received a text from G saying that he needed $40. Kayla asked him what did he need it for, but he never replied. He was so busy helping with the party he never asked her to dance or even went on the dance floor. A few minutes later, he sent the text back, so Kayla got up and went to him.

Kayla: Why do you need $40?
G: I need it for gas.
Kayla: Well, I'll have to go to the ATM after I leave here.

G: I'll take you.
Kayla: Okay.

When Kayla got back to the table, she told the girls that she rode with G and was taking her home. Once it died down, Kayla and her friends was ready to leave, so Kayla texted G to tell him she was ready to go. When they got to the door, G was standing there, talking to one of his boys. When he saw Kayla, he reached in his pocket and got the keys and reached for Kayla's hand. She immediately grabbed it, and they all walked out together. When Kayla got to G's car, he opened the door for her, and she told her friends that she would talk to them tomorrow and got in the car. G got in and started the car, and Kayla immediately looked at the gas. She noticed it was full. She didn't say anything until they got to the gas station. He pulled up to the pump and turned the car off. Kayla looked at him with a strange face.

Kayla: Are you playing me for my money?
G: For real? Seriously, you're gonna ask me that?
Kayla: Yes.
G: Why are you asking me that?
Kayla: Why can't you answer the question? I thought you said you needed it for gas.
G: I do.
Kayla: But it's full.
G: Yeah, now it is, but it won't be after I take everybody home. Why? You tripping?
Kayla: So I'm paying for you to take your people home?

They look at each other silently.

G: No, I'm not playing you for your money. I like you for real. If I didn't, you wouldn't even be in my car right now.
Kayla, not knowing if it's true: Okay.

She reached in her purse and pulled out $40 to give to him. As he reached for it, Kayla held a tight grip on it with a face that says, "Don't play with me." G tried to pull the money.

Kayla: G, I'm telling you, if I find out you used it for something else, it's gonna be a problem.
G, with a smile: I'm using it for gas, baby. I promise.

He started the car and started driving, and the whole ride to Kayla's house was plain silent, except for the radio playing. When they finally reached Kayla's house, G parked and cut the car off. Looking at Kayla and not saying anything, he put his finger on her chin and turned her face to him. He leaned over and kissed her on the lips.

G: Can I come back when I drop everybody off?
Kayla: Sure. What time do you think that will be?
G: Not sure, maybe an hour or two.
Kayla: Okay.
G: I'll be back as soon as I drop everyone off.

Kayla grabbed her purse and got out of the car. G made sure she got in the house and pulled off. Kayla went into her room and cut the light on and went to pull out one of her sexy lingerie. She cut on the shower and wrapped her hair up. Two hours after she got out of the shower, she decided to call G but didn't get an answer. Kayla went and got on the computer to help pass time until G got there. Another hour passed, and she called again but still didn't get an answer. She called and called but never got an answer. Kayla lay in her bed, mad as hell. She decided to call G one last time, and he finally answered.

G: Hello.
Kayla: Where are you?
G: I'm on my way now, baby. I'm still dropping people off, and then I'm there.

Kayla: Okay, hurry up.

G: Okay.

Kayla started lighting candles and incense for her young lover, and she was thinking about making breakfast since it was after 5:00 a.m., but she didn't. Looking at the clock, she noticed it was after 6:00 a.m. Kayla kept pacing the floor and looking out the window until she realized it was 6:30 a.m. She picked up the phone and called him, but he didn't answer. Lying in the bed, she finally fell asleep and woke up at 4:00 p.m. She reached for her phone to find out that he never called. Her face was full of anger and disappointment. She didn't call him for the rest of the day. Kayla's cousin was having a little get-together over her house later that night. Kayla's phone rang while she was talking and laughing with her family, so she answered the phone with laughter.

Kayla: Hello.

G: Hey, baby, what's good?

Kayla, with an angry voice: Nothing at all.

G: What's wrong?

Kayla: Nothing.

G: What you doing?

Kayla: Over my cuz's house party.

G: Oh yeah, can I come through?

Kayla: Sure, just like you did last night.

G: I know. I'll explain about that, but can I come?

Kayla: Yeah.

Kayla gave him the address, and like he said, he showed up. Kayla was glad he did because she wanted to see him. When he got out of the car, butterflies were in Kayla's stomach. He got out of the car and spoke to everyone whom he had met the night before, and she introduced him to everyone that he didn't meet. One of Kayla's cousin's named Aaron like to be considered as the one that tries to figure out if someone is good enough to be with someone in his family. So Aaron went over to G and Kayla and said, "Cuz, I gotta steal him away from you for a minute. You know I got to have that family talk with him."

Kayla started laughing and said, "Okay."

While they're over there talking, Kayla went back to the others to dance, talk, and have a good time. While Kayla was over there learning new dances from the kids, G slowly came behind her and grabbed her around her waist and started dancing with her. Aaron, being a DJ, changed the CD in his car to a slow jam. Everyone watched as they slow-danced. They look so cute together, everyone was saying.

As the night got late, everyone was tired and ready to go. Kayla and G said their good-nights and left. On the way to Kayla's house, G got a call from his brother. He had to go pick him up. When they picked him up, he kissed Kayla on the cheek and told G he wanted to stop by his girl's house. They stopped there and were there for over an hour. Kayla gave G the same look she had before.

Kayla: How long is your brother gonna be?
G: I don't know.
Kayla: Well, can you blow the horn? We've been waiting for a while.
G, blowing the horn: Okay.

His brother came to the car and said that he was staying there. Kayla was very angry and looked his brother dead in the eye.

Kayla: And you couldn't tell us that a long time ago.
Bro: I just decided.
Kayla, looking at G: Wow.

G backed out the driveway and drove off. Kayla was still talking about how G's brother kept them waiting that long without telling them he was staying. She could tell that G was getting agitated and frustrated hearing about it.

G: I think we gonna wait until tomorrow because it's late.

Kayla: No!
G: It's 5:00 a.m., bay.
Kayla: So that's you brother's fault.

G didn't say anything else. As he was driving, Kayla noticed that he was taking streets that he usually takes to her house. She didn't say anything, but when he pulled up in front of her house, he put the car in park but doesn't cut it off.

Kayla: So you're not coming in?
G: Bay, it's late.
Kayla: What's going on, G? Do you need to tell me something?
G: Like what?
Kayla: Something, anything you think I need to know.
G: No, but you know I'm living the single life, so there are other women, just not tonight.

Kayla was shocked when he said that. Knowing how it already was, she still felt that it was disrespectful for him to say that to her face. She didn't know how to take it or what to say. She just knew that she couldn't get mad about it. She grabbed her purse and got out of the car, slamming the door. G rolled down the window.

G: So you just gonna slam my door?

Kayla kept walking while crying, trying not to let him see or hear her. She didn't respond.

G: Okay, whatever.

Chapter Three

Kayla didn't call G anymore after they saw each other the last time. Neither did G call her. A whole month went by with them not speaking. Kayla noticed her period was late. The next morning, Kayla wasn't feeling well, so she walked into her clinic. After seeing the doctor, Kayla found out that she was pregnant. Sitting on her bed, not knowing what to do, she called her best friend, Evelyn, crying about her situation.

Kayla: Do you think I should keep it or just get rid of it?
Evelyn: Well, if it was me, I would tell him about me being pregnant and how much the abortion would cost because he ain't worth shit.

Kayla took her friend's advice and found the courage to call him.

G: Hello.
Kayla: Hi, how are you?
G: Good. What about you?
Kayla: Not too good. We need to talk.
G: Okay, what's wrong?
Kayla: Do you think you can come over here? I want to talk face-to-face.
G: Yeah, give me a couple of hours.
Kayla: Okay. Call when you're on your way.

G: Okay.

Kayla waited for three hours to pass and still no call from G. She started calling him, and he wouldn't answer the phone from that point on. G finally called Kayla the next day and asked her to bring him some chicken to his job for lunch. Kayla, being upset, told G that she wasn't bringing him shit until they talked about their situation. G didn't say anything and just hung up the phone. Kayla slowly hung up the phone and started crying. Lying in bed in her dark room, she heard a knock on the door. It was Evelyn.

Evelyn: Hey, girl. Why you sitting in the dark?
Kayla: I wasn't feeling too well.
Evelyn: What's wrong with you?

Kayla, sitting silently, just broke down and started crying. Evelyn ran over to hug her.

Kayla: It's G.
Evelyn: What did he do or not?
Kayla: I keep telling him that I need to talk to him, but he won't listen. Every time he says he's coming to talk about it, he never shows up, and time is going fast.
Evelyn: Okay, so that's when *you* do. Where is he at?
Kayla: Work.
Evelyn: Let's go.

Kayla, scared but anxious, got up, got dressed, and headed out the door behind Evelyn. At this time, he was working at a muffler shop. They pulled up in the parking lot and parked. Kayla pulled out the pregnancy test results and opened the door. Evelyn told her to relax, and she would go and get him. Evelyn went in, and she saw another worker and asked for G. When she got back in the car, she told Kayla that they sent him home early. They went to his house, but there was no answer. They made their way back to

Kayla's house. Pacing back and forth, Kayla made many attempts to call him, and once again, he never answered.

Evelyn: Here, call that nigga from my phone.

Kayla grabbed the phone and dialed his number.

G: Hello.
Kayla: So I have to call you from another phone for you to answer my call?
G: No, I've been busy.
Kayla: Well, for you to be busy, you answered the phone. Can we talk now?
G: Look, what is it about?
Kayla: I want to tell you face-to-face.
G: What's the difference if it's over the phone or face-to-face?
Kayla: Look, I'm trying to give you respect in this situation because your choice and decision do matter.
G: Okay. I'll be over there tonight.
Kayla: You promise?
G: I said I'll be there. What time you want me to come?
Kayla: I don't know, about 7:00 p.m.
G: Okay.
Kayla: Thank you.

Kayla hung up the phone and looked at Evelyn.

Kayla: Now if this nigga don't show up tonight, I'm just gonna handle it myself.
Evelyn: Uh uh, hell no, he helped you make the baby, he gonna help pay for it either way, and I'm gonna be here when he come.

It's 6:47 p.m. As they waited, they're drinking wine and talking to make the time go by fast. There's a knock at the door. Kayla jumped and looked at Evelyn. Holding the glass in her hand, she shivered and shook her head.

Evelyn: Girl, get your ass up and get the door.

Kayla got up and slowly walked to the window. Dropping her head and exhaling heavily in relief, she opened the door. It's her cousin Aaron.

Aaron: What up, doe? I drink galore as usual.
Evelyn: Hey now, how you feel?
Aaron: Sexy, now that I see you.

Everyone laughed.

Evelyn: What you drinking on?
Aaron: Whatever you want, I got it.

Aaron pulled out what seems to be every kind of liquor they sell at the store and one can of beer.

Kayla: Damn, nigga, for real? Where the party at? Because it's sure not here.
Aaron: Cuz, we are the party.
Evelyn: Well, we're supposed to have another person in about fifteen minutes ago.

Looking at her watch, Kayla notices that it's 7:15 p.m., and she excused herself from the living room and went into her bedroom.

Aaron: Who suppose to be coming?
Evelyn: G.
Aaron: Is that my man from the other night for cuz?
Evelyn: Yeah.
Aaron: Oh okay. He drink?
Evelyn, laughing: Yeah, but not like you.

Aaron: I know that's right because ain't nobody bad like me.

While Aaron and Evelyn were in the living room talking, Kayla was in her bedroom calling G. But to no surprise, there's no answer. When she hung the phone up and turned to walk out the room, the phone rang. It's G.

Kayla: Hello.
G: Open the door.

Kayla went in the living room to open the door. G walked in and spoke to everyone. Aaron offered him a drink, but he didn't accept it. Kayla and G went into Kayla's room. Evelyn went and looked out the window and saw a girl sitting in his car.

G: What's up?
Kayla: You sure have been acting funky.
G: No, I haven't. What's up? I'm in a rush.
Kayla: I thought you were gonna be here at 7:00 p.m.
G: I'm late, but I'm here now.
Kayla: Okay, here.

Kayla handed him the results.

G: What's this?
Kayla: Read it.

While G read the paper, his eyes got big. He grabbed his head and sat on Kayla's bed. Kayla, still standing with her arms folded, was wondering what he's gonna say. G stood up finally and looked at Kayla.

G: So what you gonna do?
Kayla: You mean what are we gonna do?
G: Look, I don't want it, so…

Kayla: And you think I do? I don't either, so I'm gonna find out how much the abortion is gonna cost, and I'll let you know.
G: For what?
Kayla: So you can pay half.
G: Look, I don't want to have nothing to do with it.

While G and Kayla were in the bedroom talking, there's a knock on the door. Evelyn got up to answer it, and when she did and opened the door, it's a girl asking for G.

Evelyn: Can I help you?
Girl: Is G here?
Evelyn: Well, did you see what house he went to?
Girl: Yeah, he came here.
Evelyn: So why would you ask if he was here?
Girl: Look, can you just tell him to come on, please?

Aaron stepped up to the door.

Aaron: Damn, who dis?

No one said anything. Aaron looked down at the girl's stomach.

Aaron: Oh, never mind.

She was pregnant as well. Kayla and G were still in the room talking, and it got even louder. The door opened hard and fast when G came storming out with Kayla right behind him, arguing about the situation. He looked and saw the girl.

G: What you get out the car for?
Girl: Because I have to use the bathroom.
Evelyn, laughing: You're so stressed, but I understand why. You got double trouble.
G: Do I even know you?

Evelyn: Not really, but I know about you and how you are.

Before the conversation could get any worse, Kayla opened the door so that G could leave and told him good night. Aaron, still looking confused because he doesn't know why everything happened the way it did, lifted his glass.

Aaron: That's why I drink!

Chapter Four

Kayla finally got the abortion done two weeks after her talk with G. She was upset, but she knew it was for the best. Knowing that G would not have been there for the baby made her quite confident in her decision. She still wanted to know if the other girl was pregnant by him and did she do the same thing. Several months went by without hearing from G. She would think about him at times, actually a lot, especially on weekends because that was when she saw him the most, but she would think about the age difference too. Kayla had gone out with her friends one night and met a man. His name was Tony. He was older than her, so it didn't make her uncomfortable. They dated for some time. Then he finally told her that he was married. At that time, Kayla didn't care because he was taking care of her. So basically, he was a sugar daddy. He was a retired veteran and retired from GM, so of course, he was loaded with money. Kayla had a bank account that her Tony opened for her. She had furs, clothes that filled all closets in her house, shoes and boots galore, jewelry, and everything a woman would want and have without working for it. She wasn't in love with him, so it was easy for her to be herself around him. While she was at the movies with her Tony, she got a call. She looked at the phone, and it was G. Wondering what he wanted and curious to answer the phone, she pushed the end button. After the movie was over, they went to the car and left. On their way home, Kayla decided to call G.

G: Hello.

Kayla: Yes, someone called this number.

G: Yeah, it's G. What's good witcha?

Kayla: Oh. Life.

G: That's wassup. What you doing?

Kayla: On my way home from the movies.

G: Oh, with who?

Kayla: What?

G: Who you go to the movies with?

Kayla: What do you want, G?

G: Can you stop by here for a minute?

Kayla: For what?

G: I just need you to stop by please.

Kayla: Okay, all right, I'll be there.

Hanging up the phone, slowly wondering why he wanted her to come by, she looked at Tony.

Kayla: Baby, if you don't mind, can we make a quick stop?

Tony: Sure, no problem.

She directed him which way to go. When they got there, G and some of his boys were out on the porch, looking and wondering who was in this gold-colored Hummer. When the door opened, they stood up because they didn't know what to expect. Kayla got out and started walking up to the porch, looking fabulous. As said before, even though she's older, she didn't look her age. G met her halfway. He tried to hug her, but she pushed him away.

Kayla: No.

G: Oh okay. I guess your man will be mad, huh?

Kayla didn't say anything. G went into the house with Kayla following right behind him. They entered his room.

G: So how you been?

Kayla: Good. What's going on, G?
G: Did you take care of that?
Kayla: Does it matter?
G: Well, I just need to know if I have a baby I need to take care of.
Kayla: I handled it.
G: Look, I was just going through a lot of things at that time, and it was distracting me from everything and everybody, and I just want to apologize.
Kayla: I accept, and you could've done this over the phone.
G: Maybe I just wanted to see you.
Kayla: Tonight is not a good night. I'm busy.
G: What time are you finishing up with him?
Kayla: Tomorrow. G, what do you want from me?
G: Can I see you tomorrow?
Kayla: G, look, it's been a while since I saw and talked to you, and you're out of my system, and the way you treated me was just out cold.
G: And I apologize for that.

Kayla looked at G straight in his eyes. Thinking maybe he's telling the truth and will be up front this time, she thought, *Maybe it will be better.*

Kayla: Okay, call me tomorrow.
G: Okay.

Kayla turned to walk out the room, but G grabbed her hand and pulled her to him and laid one of those soft big long lip kisses on her. When they separated, they looked at each other, and Kayla turned to walk away. As she walked to the car, Tony got out and opened the door for her. When he closed the door, she saw that all of them were looking. *Maybe these young niggas will learn a lesson on how to treat a lady*, she thought to herself. G watched as they drove away.

Chapter Five

The next day was rainy and gloomy. Kayla, woken up by an early phone call, was lying next to Tony. She hurried up and picked up the phone. When she saw who was calling, she answered it slowly, got out of the bed, and went to the bathroom. It was G.

Kayla: Why are you calling this early?
G: I was thinking about you all night. Can we go eat breakfast?
Kayla: I'm not at home right now, G.
G: Well, how about lunch? I really need to see you.
Kayla, sighing: I guess I can make it. I will call you when I'm home.
G: Okay, thank you.

When Kayla returned to the bed, she laid down thinking what she was gonna tell Tony so that he can take her home. Tony rolled over and put his arm around her.

Tony: Good morning.
Kayla: Good morning
Tony: What time is it?
Kayla: 8:00 a.m.

Tony quickly opened his eyes and looked at his watch. He hurried and got out of the bed.

Tony: Baby, I have to go. I was supposed to be home by now.
Kayla: Okay.

Kayla, getting up with a face of relief, grabbed her clothes and went into the bathroom. Slightly smiling, she got dressed, thinking everything turned out cool because she didn't have to lie. Kayla is the type of person that tries not to lie, especially to a person who's helping her. As they were walking to the car, he was explaining why he had to go. She told him that she understood, and it was okay. When they arrived at her house, he kissed her and gave her some money before she got out, and then he pulled off. It's now 9:30 a.m., and Kayla was thinking about calling G at that moment. While drinking coffee, she strolled down memory lane about her and G. Feelings that were never supposed to happen were coming back slowly. In a way, Kayla wanted to see him again. She picked up the phone and dialed his number for the first time in a while. G answered the phone when it hardly rung, as if he was waiting for her to call.

G: Hey, pooh.
Kayla, with a smile: What did you call me?
G: I said pooh.
Kayla: Oh, so now I have a nickname.
G: You deserve one.
Kayla: Oh, I feel so special.
G: You are special to me.
Kayla: I'm so confused.
G: About what?
Kayla: You.
G: Well, we can we go to a restaurant and talk about it then.
Kayla: It's not time for lunch yet.
G: Well, we can make it brunch.
Kayla, smiling: Okay, let me get dressed.
G: Okay, I'm driving, so I'm on my way.
Kayla: Okay, I'll be ready.

Kayla went into the room to find something to wear then jumped in the shower. There's a knock at the door before she's finished dressing. She opened the door, and it's G. She let him in and told him to have a seat on the couch until she finished dressing. When she walked into the living room, she heard him on the phone. When he saw her, he told them he will text them. Kayla, not worrying, said she's ready, and out the door they went. G opened the door for Kayla to get in the car, and then he got in. Before he could start the car, he got a text, read it, and responded. He then started the car. While he's driving, Kayla wondered what restaurant he was taking her to.

Kayla: So where are we going?
G: It's a surprise.

Kayla smiled, and another text came in. It seemed like this happened every five minutes. Kayla was getting upset, and she found it very disrespectful of him to be texting while they're on a lunch date, let alone while he's driving. She was curious to know who it was that he was texting, but she didn't say anything. She was trying to think of a way to find out who it was. They finally got to the restaurant. After going in and being seated, G asked Kayla if she had any hand sanitizer. Kayla, knowing that she had some, said no. G told her he was going to the bathroom and got up. He left his phone on the table, which was what Kayla was hoping for. When he went in the bathroom, Kayla hurried and grabbed the phone and went to the texts. She found out it was a girl named Trick. She didn't know if that was her real name or not, but Kayla didn't have a problem calling her that. She didn't have enough time to read it because he was coming out the door. She hurried up and placed the phone back where it was. G sat down and picked up the phone and texted again.

G: Did they ask for the orders yet?
Kayla: No. So who are you texting?
G: Oh no, baby, just one of my boys.

Kayla: Really, this early?
G: Yeah, it's always with him.

While they sat there eating, they talked and laughed. When they finished eating, Kayla just knew that G was gonna have her pay, but to her surprise, when the waiter brought the check, G picked it up, looked at it, and took money out of his wallet. Kayla was impressed. On the way home, G asked if it was okay for him to come by tonight. Kayla told him yeah, even though she knew not to prepare herself for it. They reached Kayla's house, and G cut the car off.

G: So what time would you like me to come?
Kayla: You can just call when you feel like coming.
G: You don't believe I'm coming, do you?
Kayla: It doesn't matter what I believe. If you do, you do. If not, then oh well.
G: Okay, I'll show you.

G leaned over to kiss her. He tried to French kiss her, but Kayla wouldn't let it happen. He looked at her, wondering why she's acting like that. He held her hand and told her he'll be back. Kayla got out of the car. He called for her, and she turned around and bent to the window.

G: Do you have $50?
Kayla: What?
G: Can I borrow $50?
Kayla: You still owe me $40!
G: I know. I'll pay you back.
Kayla: How did you pay for brunch?
G: That was all I had.
Kayla: Wow! Your boy doesn't have it?
G: Who?
Kayla: The one you been texting all day.
G: No, he asked me for a loan.

Kayla: Well, I don't have it.
G: You sure?
Kayla: Nigga, didn't I just say I don't have it?
G: Okay. Well, I'll be back.

Kayla turned and walked away, thinking he's definitely not coming back now. G waited for her to get in the house then pulled off. She wondered why he needed the money since he works at the muffler shop. While time was going by, she was trying to decide if she should at least find something to wear in case he does come, so she got up and pulled out a shirt and a pair of shorts and a lingerie outfit. Then she decided to give the house a good cleaning. While she was cleaning, she cooked too. She made spaghetti with garlic bread and a salad. Once she finished, she sat on the couch and looked at her watch. It was 7:30 p.m. She was going to take a shower. As soon as she got up to run a shower, the phone rang. It was G, telling her that he was at the store and on his way. Her heart jumped because she really didn't believe he was coming, but by him calling, she knew he was. So she quickly got in the shower and put on the lingerie outfit with her robe on top. She heard a knock on the door. She put on her slippers and went to the window and saw that it was G. She opened up the door and invited him in.

G: Hey, pooh.
Kayla: Hey. What's that in your hand?
G: Just a bottle of wine.
Kayla: Oh, how thoughtful. I have some spaghetti, garlic bread, and salad. Would you like a plate?
G: Hell yeah, hook me up, pooh.

G had a seat on the couch. While his food was warming up, Kayla filled the ice bucket up and came out with two wine glasses and lit the candles. G was looking at her up and down with those sexy bedroom eyes. Kayla saw him.

Kayla: What's wrong?

G: Nothing. Why you ask me that?

Kayla: Because you're looking at me the way you did when I first met you.

G: Oh no, I was just thinking about the first time we made love.

Kayla, shocked: That wasn't making love. That was fucking.

G: It might have been a fuck to you.

Kayla, confused and staring at him and talking slowly: Oh.

They stared at each other. The microwave dinged, and Kayla went and brought G his plate. He started eating and moaning, telling her how well it was. Kayla poured them some wine. As he ate, they hold a conversation. G was finally finished eating, so he sat the plate on the table and pulled out a cigarette. Kayla got up and took the plate out and brought him a paper towel. While he sat there, wiping his mouth, Kayla felt the wine kicking in. She started staring at him but trying not to let him notice she's looking at his eyes, wanting to get undressed because she's ready. He's talking and laughing, and then he noticed that Kayla wasn't.

G: What's wrong, pooh?

Kayla, shaking her head and speaking softly: Nothing.

G, laughing: I know what's wrong. You feeling good.

Kayla, smiling: Yeah, a little. I like it when you call me that.

G: What?

Kayla: Pooh.

G: Well, you are my pooh.

Kayla: Well, I'm gonna make you my poppy.

G, smiling: That's cute.

Kayla: Well, I decided since you did show up, you deserve a nickname. And besides, it's something about them eyes, boy.

G, laughing: What, they red?

Kayla: No, you have bedroom eyes.

G: Well, if that's the case, maybe they should be in the bedroom.

G stared at her with smoke mingling in the air. He sat up and put the cigarette out. He started staring back at her, and she stared at him. He got up and took her by the hand. She led him to the bedroom. Before they could even make it in all the way, G turned her around, dropped to his knees, and gave her what she been wanting with those lips of his. Going faster and faster, he got more aggressive. Putting both her legs around his shoulders, he made his way to the bed. Laying her back on the bed while his lips seem glued to her pussy, he grabbed her tits. Kayla grabbed him by the head and told him that she wants it hard and rough. He started kissing up her stomach and made his way to her lips. Kayla, fighting her way to unbuckle his pants so she can suck his dick, tried to roll him over. As they're still kissing, he stopped and went down on her again. Kayla went crazy. She wrapped her legs around his head to make sure he can't move, but he didn't try to. As Kayla's moans got louder, she pulled on the comforter and lifted her ass all the way up in the air with G's head following her every move. Faster and faster, she moved her ass in the air as she reached her climax, slowing down her movement as she returned her ass back to the bed, G finally came out of the pussy and lay next to Kayla. Kayla, smiling, put her hand around G's dick and stroked up and down as she slid her body down. With her face right in front of his dick, she started licking it while stroking. G was watching her as she teases his dick. She stroked faster and faster then quickly wrapped her mouth around his fat long dick. G started moaning loud and grabbing Kayla's hair. Kayla started sucking his dick faster because he's rubbing her nipples, making them hard. All of a sudden, G did a loud grunt, and the release of nut was all over her mouth. G watched as she swallowed and licked her lips. Lifting her and placing her faced down on her bed, G began to lick her body slowly from the bottom going up. Moaning heavily, Kayla lay there, still with her eyes closed. Massaging her ass with his hands, he pushed his dick in her pussy. Going in and out, he clutched on to her hands. It didn't take long for her to have another orgasm, and he was on his way, but Kayla told him to stop because she wanted to go for a ride. He lay on his back and Kayla got up and put his dick in her pussy. Wildly, she started moving on his dick. Loud moans and groans were coming from them both. G grabbed Kayla's tits and squeezed them hard enough to make her scream. He pulled Kayla down to him, lying chest to chest, and he bounced up and down into her pussy. Kayla broke away and came back up to take control again. Bouncing and rolling all around, she made him release while squeezing her thigh. Falling next to G, they both lay there breathing heavily and laughing.

Kayla: You okay?
G: I should be asking you that.

G got up and put on his pants then lay on the bed and stayed there for a while. At that moment, Kayla decided to takes a shower. When she finished, she went back to the room to find G asleep. Not knowing if she should wake him up or let him sleep, she lay on his chest and looked at him thinking, *I can't believe I did this shit again. I keep falling for this shit, but hopefully, it won't be like it was before. He looks so nice and innocent but wants to live the single life. I wish I could have a real relationship with him. But still, he's too damn young. Damn, he looks and smells good. He knows how to dress, and that dick is the bomb. Okay, pull it together, Kayla. You can't let your guard down again.*

It's been said that men aren't really ready to settle down until they're in their thirties and sometimes not even then. Kayla wanted to tell G how she feels, but she doesn't want to scare him away. She decided to wake him up to see if he wanted to leave.

Kayla: G? It's 1:00 a.m.
G: Okay. Wake me up at 3:00 a.m.
Kayla: Okay.

While Kayla lay there trying to remember everything that happened there that night, she heard G's cell phone ring. She wanted to see who it was that's calling, but his phone was on the belt of his pants that he had on. She tried to push the silent button, but it kept ringing. He lay still as the phone kept ringing. She pulled it out the case and got out the bed to go into the bathroom. She looked at the phone and found out that it was Trick. While she had the phone, she thought she would go through the texts. Before she can start reading it, the phone rang again. Thinking if she should answer it or not, she pushed the silent button and held the phone tightly. She answered the phone, pushed mute, and put the phone up to her ear.

Trick, hollering: Hello? Hello? G? G?

The phone hung up. Kayla was still holding the phone because she knew she was gonna call back. As Kayla knew, the phone rang. Kayla repeated the same thing that she did last time.

Trick: Hello? Hello? G, stop playing. Hello?

The phone hung up again. Kayla told herself that she was gonna answer the phone the next time she called. She looked out the door and went in the hallway to see if G was still asleep, and he was. She ran back in the bathroom and closed the door. The phone rang, and she answered before it could stop ringing.

Kayla, with a sleepy voice: Hello.
Trick: Who is this?
Kayla: Who is this?
Trick: Put G on the phone.
Kayla: Who's calling?
Trick: What?
Kayla: Who's calling?
Trick: Where is G?
Kayla: He's sleep. Who are you?
Trick: I'm G's woman
Kayla: No, you're not because if he had a woman, he wouldn't be here with me in my bed asleep.

Trick hung the phone up in Kayla's face. Kayla couldn't believe what just happened, knowing that G would be mad when Trick tells him what happened. Kayla turned off G's phone and returned to the room. She got in bed and turned over to see that it was 3:10 a.m. She didn't know if she wanted to wake him up because she knew he was going to look at his phone. But she woke him up, and he told her to wake him up at 6:00 a.m. Kayla went to sleep with a smile after kissing him on the cheek.

Chapter Six

I t's the next morning and the smell of spring filled the room. The sun was shining bright on Kayla's face. She woke up to see that it's 8:00 a.m. She turned around to wake G up, but all she saw was a note: "Pooh, I locked both bottom locks of the doors. I tried to wake you up, but you slept so peacefully I couldn't disturb you. I'll call you later." Kayla held the note smiling, but the smile faded away when she remembered the phone call and what she did. Besides, she wanted to see if he would make the first move, but she knew it wasn't gonna happen. Kayla got up and made herself some coffee and went to the computer. She logged on to Facebook and put her status up that said, "Last night was one of the best nights I ever had." About five minutes after that, Evelyn called.

Kayla: Hey, girl.
Evelyn: Damn, girl, you up early.
Kayla: Yeah, I know.
Evelyn: So uh, what happened last night?
Kayla: Nothing.
Evelyn: Girl, bye, I read your status. So what's up with that?
Kayla, laughing: Okay.

Kayla told Evelyn what happened from beginning to end.

Evelyn: Well, you just be careful. You don't want it to be like it was last time.

Kayla: Yeah, I know.

Evelyn: Did y'all use a rubber.

Kayla: Huh?

Evelyn: Bitch, you didn't, did you?

Kayla: We wasn't thinking about it.

Evelyn: Girl, if it happens again, I'm kicking yours and his ass. Please believe me.

Kayla believed her because Evelyn is the type of person that believes in doing the right thing even if it's wrong. They talked for a little while longer and got off the phone. Kayla got up and pulled out a pair of jeans and a T-shirt to wear today. The phone rang. It was Tony, inviting Kayla to lunch. She was really tired, and her legs hurt, but she agreed to go because he done so much for her. She felt like she was obligated. So she put back the jeans and T-shirt and pulled out casual clothes. She went and freshened up and did her hair. She heard the horn blow, so she grabbed her purse and got out the house. She got in the car and gave Tony a kiss.

Kayla: Hey.

Tony: Hey, baby. You okay?

Kayla: Yeah, why you ask me that?

Tony: You look tired, and the way you were walking…

Kayla: Oh, my legs been hurting me from doing my exercises.

Tony: Oh, you need anything?

Kayla: No, baby, I'm okay, but thanks anyway.

Tony: Anything for my baby.

As they drove, they decided to go to a Mexican restaurant. Kayla only ate a salad because she really wasn't that hungry. After that, Tony wanted to catch a movie. All Kayla could think about at the movies was G and the sex they had last night. After the movie, Tony was hungry again, so they went to the restaurant of Kayla's choice, and she chose Red Lobster. But on the way to Red Lobster,

Kayla wanted to make a stop at a tattoo shop. They finally made it to the restaurant after an hour. While they were sitting there waiting to order, Kayla got a text from G. "Last night was fun. I forgot how good that pussy was. We have to do it again tonight." Kayla's heart jumped. He did exactly what she wanted him to. Tony was talking, but Kayla wasn't listening to a word he was saying. She was too busy smiling and thinking. All of a sudden, her phone rings. It's G. Kayla excused herself from the table and went into the restroom, but by the time she made it there, it stopped. She's scared to call him back because of her and Trick's conversation. But she did.

G: Hey, pooh.
Kayla: Hey.
G: Where you at?
Kayla: Dinner.
G: With who?
Kayla: Tony.
G: Oh okay. Are we on for tonight?
Kayla: Yeah.
G: What time?
Kayla: I don't know. Just call when you're on your way.
G, laughing: You still don't trust me, do you?
Kayla, laughing: I didn't say that.
G: Okay, I'll call you.
Kayla: Okay, bye.

Kayla returned to the table with Tony. She felt so bored, and she's so ready to go. She tried to think of something to say or do so that he can take her home. Kayla grabbed her stomach.

Kayla: Ow.
Tony: You're okay?
Kayla: Yeah, I just feel a little pain.
Tony: You need to go to the hospital?
Kayla: No, that's okay. Ow!

Tony: You sure you don't need to go to the hospital?
Kayla: No, I think I just need to lie down.
Tony: Want me to take you home?
Kayla: If you don't mind.
Tony: Not at all.

Tony waved for the waiter to bring the check. He held her as they walked to the car. He opened the door and put her in. They arrived in front of Kayla's house, and Tony parked and cut the car off.

Tony: Do you need any help?
Kayla: No, baby, you did enough. Listen, I want to apologize for ruining dinner.
Tony: No, no, baby, it's okay. I could tell something was wrong. Why didn't you tell me you didn't feel good?
Kayla, holding her stomach: I didn't want to disappoint you.
Tony: Okay, baby, go ahead and get in the house.
Kayla: Okay.

Kayla leaned over and gave him a goodbye kiss. As she got out of the car, closed the door, and turned around to walk to the house, she felt bad. But at the same time, she's glad she's back at home. As soon as Kayla got in the house, the phone rang. She saw that it's Evelyn and decided not to answer the phone. Instead, she said she will call her after she settles down. After changing her clothes and getting comfortable, she picked the phone up and called Evelyn.

Evelyn: Hey, girl, I just called you.
Kayla: I know that's why I'm calling back.
Evelyn: What you doing?
Kayla: Nothing. Just got in.
Evelyn: Where you been?
Kayla: Out with Tony.
Evelyn: Oh, where y'all go?

Kayla: Girl, we went to breakfast, then to the movies, and then out to dinner. I was so ready to go home. I acted like I was sick.

Evelyn: That's bold.

Kayla: I know. I feel so bad.

Evelyn: I bet if it was G, you wouldn't have done that.

They both started laughing.

Kayla: Yeah, true that. But guess what?

Evelyn: What?

Kayla: While we were at dinner, G texted me and said he forgot how good the pussy was, and he wants to be with me again tonight.

Evelyn: Hell no, girl, you need to leave him alone.

Kayla: Why?

Evelyn: Because he playing you.

Kayla: Playing me for what? I don't have anything.

Evelyn: Money! Didn't you give him money?

Kayla: Girl, that was pennies.

Evelyn: Okay, I was just trying to warn you because I been there and done that.

Kayla: I got this.

Evelyn: Okay, well, call me and let me know how it goes.

Kayla: Okay.

Kayla hung up the phone and read G's text again. She noticed that he sent another text that read, "We need to talk." She wondered if it was gonna be about the conversation with Trick again. She thought if she should call him or wait for him to call her. She walked around the house, trying to find something to do to take her mind off it. She sat at her computer and got on Facebook. She checked her messages, and one of them was from G. She didn't even know that he had a Facebook account. It read, "Call me ASAP," and she saw that he left that message twenty minutes ago. Her stomach was filled with butterflies. Now she knew that he wanted her to call. Kayla was thinking of what to say in case he did ask her about talking to Trick. She finally got the courage to call him.

G: Hello.

Kayla: Hey, you wanted me to call? What's wrong? Don't tell me you're not coming, right?

G: Oh no, I'm still coming, but I need to ask you something. Did you talk to a girl named Trick last night?

Kayla: Well, I'm not gonna lie. Yes, I did.

G: What happened?

Kayla: Well, she kept calling your phone, and I didn't want her to wake you up, so I answered the phone and told her you were asleep.

G: What else?

Kayla, talking slow: She asked me who I was, and I asked her who was she, and she told me you was her man, and I told her if you was her man, you wouldn't be with me, and she hung up the phone. Please don't be mad at me.

G: Wow, no, I'm not mad, but please don't answer my phone no more.

Kayla: Okay, so is she your woman?

G: No, she's my ex. Remember, I told you me and my girl just broke up. She's her. I told you I was living the single life.

Kayla: Okay, well, when you come, I have a surprise for you.

G: What is it?

Kayla: You'll see.

G: I like surprises. I was thinking maybe you should come here this time.

Kayla: Okay, I can do that, but how am I going to get there?

G: Oh yeah, your car still down, and my brother have mine. If he be here before you're ready, I'll come get you.

Kayla: Okay, so I'll call you when I'm ready.

G: Okay, bye.

Kayla: Bye.

Kayla was happy because it turned out the way it did. She got up and picked out an outfit for the night.

It's now 9:00 p.m., and Kayla decided to start getting dressed. While she's in the shower, G called her. By the time she got out of the shower, got dressed, and did her hair, it was 10:00 p.m. She picked up her phone and called him back.

G: Hey, pooh.
Kayla: Hey.
G: Are you ready?
Kayla: Yeah, I am now. I just finished getting ready.
G: Okay, you ready for me to come get you now?
Kayla: Yeah, you can.
G: Okay, I'm on my way.
Kayla: Okay.

Kayla hurried and got everything together. Fifteen minutes later, a horn blew. She looked out the window to see G in front of the house with a car behind him. She turned off the lights in the house and turned on the porch light, made sure everything is locked, and went to get in the car. When she got in, she gave G a kiss.

Kayla: Hey, poppy, who is that behind us?
G: I don't know. They was already here.
Kayla: Oh, okay.

They started driving. On the way to G's house, he stopped at the corner store for drinks. While G was in the store, Kayla noticed the car that was in front of her house was now at the store. When G got back in the car, she told him. But he didn't worry about it. They got to the house and went in. The house was empty with no one there. They went to his room and sat on the bed. G stepped out to get glasses filled with ice and started making their drinks. There was a knock on the door. G opened the door, and there are about eight of his boys coming in. The living room was filled with nothing but niggas that quick. He came back in the room, closed the door, and put on DVD of a comedy movie. While they're sitting there, drinking and laughing, there's a knock on his bedroom door. It's one of his friends asking for a drink. His name was Sam. He looked at Kayla's skirt; it's black with fishnet trimming going down the side of her legs. He started singing Morris Day's, "Fishnet" song. Everyone started laughing and looking. G looked and said, "I didn't even see that shit." All that could be heard was some of his boys saying, "Damn."

G: All right, niggas, y'all looking too hard. It's time for y'all to go.

G closed the door, but before he could close it all the way, Sam asked if she had any friends. She told him about Evelyn. He asked her to call her.

Evelyn: Hello.
Kayla: Hey, girl, what you doing?
Evelyn: Nothing, watching TV.
Kayla: One of G's friends wants to meet you.
Evelyn: Who?
Kayla: His name is Sam.
Evelyn: Send me a picture.
Kayla: Okay.

Kayla told Sam that she wanted to see a picture of him, so he struck a pose. She sent her the picture, and quickly, she called back.

Kayla: Yeah?
Evelyn: Girl, hook it up.
Kayla: Okay.

They both started laughing and hung up. Kayla told Sam that Evelyn wanted to meet him. He told her that they could meet tomorrow. G closed the door and sat back next to Kayla. He went back to looking at her skirt. He rubbed the fishnet trimming.

G, while looking in her eyes: Damn, girl, you about to start some shit with that skirt on.

He leaned over to kiss her. They continued to watch TV and drink. A few hours later, Kayla had to use the bathroom. He showed her where it is and went back into the room. On the way to her seat, she tripped over G's shoe but did not fall.

G, laughing: You okay, pooh? You drunk?
Kayla, laughing: Yeah, and not yet.
G: But almost, right?
Kayla: Maybe. Maybe not.

Kayla took another drink, and G started rubbing her thigh and kissing her cheek up to her neck. Kayla started pushing him away and telling him to stop because she knew how she is and what will happen, but she wasn't ready yet. G sat back and started drinking again because Kayla kept pushing his hand away. Kayla turned and looked at G. He looked like he's drunk or tipsy. Kayla put her cup on the table and turned back to him.

Kayla: You are one fine young motherfucker.
G, looking at Kayla smiling: Thank you. You feeling good ain't
         you?
Kayla: Hell yeah.
G: I can make you feel better.
Kayla: How?

G put his glass on the table and turned the light out. Rubbing on Kayla's leg, he reached over to kiss her again. This time, Kayla kissed him back. While kissing, Kayla unbuckled his pants and pulled out that big dick. Separating her lips from his, she went down and wrapped her lips around his dick and started sucking.

G moaned, and he moaned even louder while she was sucking and playing with his balls. After pleasing him with her mouth, Kayla sat back on his bed. G pulled her skirt up and rubbed her tits. Kayla told him to take her panties off, and he did. He threw her panties on the floor and opened her legs wide as hell and then thrust his face into her pussy. Kayla jumped and moaned because she wasn't expecting it so suddenly. She grabbed and rubbed his head. She came fast and tried to push his head away from her pussy, but he grabbed her hand and continued. All of a sudden, he got up and turned the light on. He saw the piercing on her clit.

G: When did you get that?

Kayla: Earlier today. This was the surprise I was telling you about. You like?

G: No! Why did you get it?

Kayla: I always wanted one.

G: You should have asked me first.

Kayla: Why?

G: Because I would've told you not to get it.

Kayla, pulling him to her: Well, it's too late now, poppy.

G: Actually, it's not. You can take it out.

Kayla: Come on, poppy. You messing up the mood.

G, looking at her with a serious face, allowed her to pull him to her. She took his finger and put it in her mouth, sucking it. He started rubbing her nipple. Kayla returned to sucking his dick. G grabbed her head and hair and pulled it back and forth, controlling her movement. Pushing her head closer to his body fast, Kayla gagged, but she continued to suck. He made her gag again, and she still continued to suck. He knew she didn't want him doing it, but he did it again anyway.

Kayla: Why do you keep doing that?

G: Doing what?

Kayla: Pushing my head hard and making me gag.

G didn't say anything. Instead, he told her to get on her knees, and she did. With no touching on the ass or anything, G plunged his dick into her pussy hard, causing her to grunt. He continued to do it hard while she tells him to stop. He started hitting her on her ass hard with his hand, causing her to moan louder. Getting ready to release, he moaned but stopped his movement. Kayla thought he was done and was getting ready to get up, but he grabbed her around the waist and pushed his dick in her ass. Kayla screamed, trying to fight back, but he pushed her down on her stomach and kept fucking her in the ass hard. Kayla's yelling and crying, telling him to stop. There's a knock on the door.

G, yelling: Get the fuck away from my door!

G continued to fuck her harder and harder as Kayla's screams kept getting louder and louder. G made a strong grunt. Suddenly, G's movement slowed down. He pulled his dick out of her ass, stood up, and pulled up his pants. Kayla lay there crying and scared to move because of the pain. G opened and closed the door and argued with his boys for knocking on the door. Kayla finally found the courage to get up, but she didn't sit down. G came in, picked up his cup, and watched Kayla pick up her clothes. She got dressed and grabbed her purse.

G: Where you going?

Kayla didn't say anything. She opened up the bedroom door and walked out.

G, with a loud voice: Where you going?
Kayla, jumped and still crying: Home.
G, grabbing her hand: Look, I didn't mean for any of this to happen. It's just that a piercing on the pussy is unattractive to me. Can you please take it out? Please?

Kayla pulled her hand away and went out of the bedroom, all of his boys stared at her and shook their heads. She opened the front door and went out to call her cab. G followed right behind her. G's looking at her as if he was sorry for what happened. No one said anything the whole time they were outside. The cab finally pulled up.

G: Call me when you get home.

Kayla was getting in the cab very slow, and she didn't say anything to G. When Kayla got home, she went and ran water for a shower. She sat on her bed slowly, thinking about what just happened and why the piercing made him so upset. She got in the shower and let the water run down her back. She never called G after getting home that night. He called her, but she didn't answer the phone. He called so much that she turned her phone off. After showering, she lay in her bed and cried herself to sleep.

Chapter Seven

T he next morning, Kayla was lying in her bed. Thinking if she would be in pain because of what happened the night before, she lay there. Finally, she sat up with just a little pain in her legs. She's surprised because she thought that it would be too painful to do anything because of all the pain that G caused her. She picked up her phone to check for missed calls and found that Evelyn and G called. She started her day off with making coffee and getting on Facebook. She was going to put up a status, but she remembered that G gets on there also, so she just said, "Good morning, FB family." The phone rang, and it's Evelyn.

Kayla: Hey, girl.
Evelyn: Hey. You just getting up or something?
Kayla: No. Why?
Evelyn: I told you to call me.
Kayla: I know, girl. I had a long night.
Evelyn: What happened?

Kayla, not knowing if she really wanted Evelyn to know what happened, went ahead and told her what G did.

Evelyn: So basically he raped you?
Kayla: Girl, no, he was just mad.

Evelyn:	Call it what you want to, but it was rape to me. So anyway, about his boy, Sam, how old is he?
Kayla:	Thirty-four.
Evelyn:	Oh, that's not bad. So when did he say he wanted to meet?
Kayla:	Tonight, but I'm not going.
Evelyn:	What you mean? You have to go. I can't go by myself.
Kayla:	I don't want to see G tonight.
Evelyn:	Okay. Well, can we just meet at your place?
Kayla:	I'll see.
Evelyn:	Well, call him and see if he wants to do that and let me know.
Kayla:	And how am I supposed to do that? I don't have his number. I'll have to call G and ask him to call him.
Evelyn:	Okay. Well, call him and call me back.
Kayla:	Okay.

They hung up. Kayla, not really wanting to call G, went to the missed calls log and called him.

G:	Hello.
Kayla:	Yeah, you called?
G:	Yeah, I just wanted to see how you were doing.
Kayla:	I'm fine.
G:	Look, that shit that happened last night was just unnecessary, and I'm sorry. I don't know what happened. I just flipped out on you. I felt bad all night, and my boys were asking me questions I didn't even have the answers to. Do you forgive me?

Kayla remained silent.

G:	Hello.
Kayla:	Yeah, I'm here.
G:	Did you hear me?
Kayla:	Yeah, I heard you, but I wasn't listening.

G: What that mean?

Kayla: What is it about the piercing that made you mad?

G: I don't want to talk about it, but Sam wanted to know about your girl meeting him tonight.

Kayla: That's funny. Evelyn just asked me about meeting him.

G: Okay, that's wassup. What time y'all talking?

Kayla: I'll ask her. I'm getting my car fixed today, so I'll be able to drop her off.

G: What you mean? You're not staying?

Kayla: No, not this time.

G: Pooh, why not? We can make it a double date.

Kayla: I need to rest my ass.

G: I apologize for that. What more can I do?

Kayla: Nothing. I'll call you back.

She hung up the phone and called Evelyn.

Evelyn: Yeah?

Kayla: They said it's a go.

Evelyn: Okay, so what are you wearing?

Kayla: Well, I'm just dropping you off, and I'm leaving.

Evelyn: No, you're not. You have to stay with me at least till I feel comfortable with him.

Kayla: Okay. I'll be ready to go about 9:00 p.m.

Evelyn: See you then.

She lay in the bed for a while until it was time to get ready to go. She was thinking about calling Tony since she haven't talked to him today.

Tony: Hello.

Kayla: Hey, how you doing?

Tony: Fine. How are you doing?

Kayla: I'm feeling better.

Tony: Glad to hear that. Do you need anything?

Kayla, forgetting the dates: Well, you can bring me some soup.

Tony: On my way.

They hung up the phone. Kayla looked at the time and noticed it was kind of close to getting ready, and she knew if he came, he would want to stay for a while, so she called him back.

Tony: Yeah, baby?
Kayla: Hey, baby, I found some, so you don't have to go out of your way.
Tony: Well, I can still come and keep you company.
Kayla: I really don't feel like getting up.
Tony: Okay. Well, go ahead and rest yourself and don't hesitate to call me if you need anything.
Kayla: Okay and thank you.

Kayla got up and made her some soup. While she was cooking, there was a knock at the door. She looked out the window. It was Evelyn.

Kayla: Girl, what you doing here?
Evelyn: I figured since I wasn't doing anything at home, I'd just come here and wait for Sam unless we go over there.
Kayla: We going over there.
Evelyn: Okay.

So they sat there and talked, watched TV, and did whatever they could do to kill time. Kayla got up to go and get ready. Kayla's phone rang, and it was G.

Kayla: Hello.
G: Hey, pooh.
Kayla: Hey.
G: I need a favor.
Kayla: What?
G: I need $130. Can you help me out?
Kayla: For what?

G: I need it for something important.

Kayla: What?

G: Look, I'll explain all that after I get it and take care of this business.

Kayla: Well, I don't have it. I got my car fixed, remember?

G: Is there anyone you can borrow it from?

Kayla: No.

G: Okay. What time y'all coming?

Kayla: I'm getting ready now, so in about another hour.

G: Okay, I'll let Sam know.

They hung up the phone. And of course, Kayla told Evelyn about the conversation. Kayla continued to get dressed. Evelyn's putting finishing touches on her makeup. It's 9:00 p.m., and they're on their way out the door. While they're in the car, Kayla got another call from G.

Kayla: Yeah.

G: Hey, instead of coming here, do y'all want to get a room? We can play cards and get out drink on. Then they can leave and do their own thing.

Kayla: That's cool. I'll see what she wants to do.

Kayla told Evelyn how they wanted to do it, and she agreed to it if Sam is cool and someone she wants to be cool with. So they made their way to G's house. G and Sam were out on the porch waiting. Kayla and Evelyn got out of the car. They meet halfway, and Kayla introduced Evelyn and Sam to each other, and then she introduced her to G.

Evelyn: No wonder my girl is so into you. You look like Martin Lawrence.

G: That's what everybody says.

G came and hugged Kayla, but she didn't hug him back. He knew she was still kind of upset about the other night. As they stood there talking, G got a call, so he went in the house. When he came out, he said he had to make a stop on the way to the room. Everyone got in the cars, but Kayla rode with G, and Evelyn drove Kayla's car with Sam in the passenger side. When they got to the barber shop, which was the stop G had to make, G and Sam went in. G's phone rang, and Kayla picked it up and saw that it was Trick. She was thinking about answering it, but she didn't. Evelyn called Kayla.

Kayla: Hey.
Evelyn: Hey, what you think he had to stop for?
Kayla: Girl, I don't even know, but I'll find out. Guess what?
Evelyn: What?
Kayla: That girl Trick called G a minute ago. I think I'm gonna answer it next time and just put it back where he had it.
Evelyn, laughing: Hell naw. But what if she doesn't call?
Kayla, laughing: Then I'll just call her and put it down. I know she'll answer it. That way, she'll hear the whole conversation.
Evelyn: Girl, you crazy. Well, call because here they come.

They hang up the phone before they saw them, and Kayla pushed Trick's number and put the phone down. G gets in the car.

Kayla: So why did you have to stop here?
G: I owed somebody some money. Remember when I asked you for the money?
Kayla: Yeah.
G: That's what I needed it for.
Kayla: Oh. Who did you owe?
G, laughing: My cousin. Why you asking all these questions?
Kayla: I just wanted to know.
G: Well, now you know.

They drove to Telegraph and 7 Mile, talking all kind of talk. Kayla started talking about what she's gonna do to him sexually, and that made him talk about it too. They stopped at a liquor store. G and Sam went in. Evelyn called Kayla again.

Kayla: Yeah.

Evelyn: Did you find out?

Kayla: Yeah, he said he owed his cousin some money.

Evelyn: Oh. Did you call her?

Kayla, not being able to talk: Yep.

Evelyn: Is she still on there?

Kayla: Yep, but, girl, I can't wait till he put them big sexy lips on this pussy. Girl, that shit be feeling so good. He always talking about how my pussy is the best he ever had.

Evelyn, laughing: Girl, you are crazy, but I don't blame what you doing.

Kayla: "He gone learn today"!!!

Evelyn, laughing: Yes, he is.

Kayla: I'll call you when he finishes breaking my back.

Evelyn: Girl, shut up. Bye.

They hang up. Not too long after that, they came out. G got back in the car.

G: Do want to just go back to the house?

Kayla: I don't care.

G: Call your girl and see what she want to do.

Kayla called Evelyn and asked her, and she said she doesn't care. They decided to go back to G's house. Kayla wasn't too thrilled about it, but she just went with the flow of things, although she had a feeling something was going to go wrong. They get to the house, and G pulled his car into the driveway with Evelyn right behind him. He and Sam went into the house and brought the card table and chairs and set it up in the driveway, and G went to get these big-ass garage lights that he used when he work on cars at night. Then he went and opened all the doors to his car and put on one of his CDs. They started playing cards. *Everything was good,*

Kayla thought. A few more of G's boys pulled up, and they joined the little gathering that was now what you can say a party. At that point, G got hungry and told Kayla that he wanted some Coney Island. She gave him $20, and he asked if she did want something, she said no, but Evelyn wanted french fries, and she told Kayla that she needed to eat something too because they were all drinking, so Kayla got french fries too. G went around asking everybody if they did want anything. G and his brother left to go get the food. When he came back, he didn't give Kayla any change back. Kayla didn't know she was paying for everyone's food, but she didn't care. It was petty change to her. Then all of a sudden, something strange happened.

G: What happened to the $20 for the food?
Kayla: I don't know. I gave it to you.
G: I'm missing $20.
Kayla: Well, I don't have it. Ask one of your boys.

G sat down at the table, and the game started again. G's phone kept ringing, and he kept sliding it to Sam. Evelyn looked at the phone and saw that it was Trick. This was the same girl that Kayla had the conversation with. After a few more calls from her came, G grabbed the phone and went in the house. Kayla and Evelyn looked at each other. G was in the house for about twenty minutes. Evelyn had to use the bathroom, so Sam showed her where it was. When she came out, she told Kayla that G was on the porch, and he looked like he was mad. Kayla got up to go see what was wrong.

Kayla: G, what's wrong?
G: Just leave me alone.
Kayla: What's going on?
G: Just leave me the fuck alone.
Kayla: Look, we were just having a good time and…

G got up and got in Kayla's face.

G: Didn't I just say leave me the fuck alone?

Kayla, already drunk, got mad and knocked his phone and drink out of his hand and turned and walked back to the table. G came behind her and pushed her into his car, grabbed her, and laid her on the ground.

G: What the fuck did I tell you, huh?
Kayla: I gave you the $20.
G: Didn't I tell you to leave me the fuck alone?

Evelyn came and grabbed G's arm.

G: Get your fucking hands off me.

Kayla's on the ground holding her hands in front of her face, not knowing if he was gonna try to hit her or not. Sam finally got G off Kayla, and they went in the house. Kayla got up, crying, and went to her car. G's in there, telling everybody what happened. After he told his story, he went outside and went up to Kayla and grabbed her by the hand. She pulled her hand away.

G: Pooh, I'm sorry, but you knew that it was other girls that's why I can't understand why you're mad. You got a sugar daddy.
Kayla: I understand that it's other girls, G, but damn, can you respect me enough to let them know that I'm here and you're unavailable? You didn't even have to answer the phone, and then I tried to comfort you, and you wouldn't let me. You pushed me on the ground, G. Does that bitch know about me, G?
G: Yes, she does.
Kayla: Yeah, sure she does.

Kayla turned her back on G. He took his finger and stuck it in her pussy from the back. It felt good to her at first, but remembering what just happened made her push him away, and she walked back to the table with Evelyn.

Evelyn: Are you okay?
Kayla, wiping her face: Yeah.
Evelyn, putting her arm around Kayla: Do you want to go?
Kayla: No, I'm good.

Sam came and sat at the table and asked Kayla the same thing, and she gave him the same answer. They sat there trying to figure what made G so mad. G came and sat at the table and just stared at Kayla. Kayla tried to avoid looking at him by talking with Evelyn and Sam. G then stood up and said, "Come here, pooh". Kayla looked at Evelyn and went to walk behind G. They went in the house and to his room. G closed the door and started kissing Kayla and tried to pull her pants down. Kayla was kissing him back at first then pushed him.

Kayla: What made you mad, G?
G, kissing Kayla: I don't want to talk about it.
Kayla: We need to talk.
G: We can talk after I get some of this.
Kayla: Can we wait till we get to the room?
G: We can still do it at the room.
Kayla: Come on now, let's talk.
G, giving Kayla a crazy look: We can talk later.

G opened the door and walked out. The night was late, about 3:00 a.m. Everything died down, and Evelyn was ready to go. Kayla told G she was getting ready to go. G, knowing Kayla was drunk, decided that he will drive Evelyn home in Kayla's car. Kayla fell asleep while G was driving, but Evelyn was awake. Evelyn was giving G directions to her house, but he told her he had to make a stop. He stopped at a building where they have swingers parties at, and this girl pulled up across him, facing the other way. It was Trick.

G: I told you to wait till I get here

Trick: I got tired of waiting on you. You should have been here.

The two just looked at each other. Kayla decided to wake up, and she sat up to see who G was talking to. All of a sudden, Trick screeched off in her raggedy car. Kayla sat back, and G started driving again. Kayla fell back to sleep. They finally got to the stop where Evelyn wanted to be dropped off at. Kayla woke up and gave Evelyn a hug and told her she will call her later on. G started driving again. Kayla questioned G about going to see some other girl while driving her car.

Kayla: So who was the girl you went to see in my car, G?

G: Just a friend.

Kayla: Why you go see her in my car? That's so fucking disrespectful. Why couldn't you use your car after I left?

G: I figured I was doing you a favor driving your girl home, so I made a stop. What's the big deal?

Kayla: Who was she? Was it Trick?

G: No.

Kayla didn't say anything else. They made it back to his house. He cut the car off and made a call. He told them to come on. While he was waiting, he took the bag with the drinks and the cigarettes in the house. Five minutes later, the same car that was at the swinger party pulled in his driveway. A girl got out, and G came out of the house. They both went up to Kayla's car.

G: Kayla, this Trick. Trick, Kayla.

Kayla spoke, but Trick said nothing.

G: This is the woman I love, and we can't do this anymore.

Kayla: I thought you were single and living the single life, at least that's what you told me.

G: I was at the time but not anymore.

Kayla: Okay, that's fine. Can I get my money back?
G: I don't have it.
Kayla: Does Trick have it?
G: No.
Kayla: Okay.

As G and Trick turned to walk away, Kayla got out of her car, closed the door, and busted G in the back of his head. She walked around to get in the car, and she heard Trick tell him, "Just come on, keep walking."

Kayla repeated what she said, "Yeah, that's right, G. Do what your bitch said and keep walking in the house."

Sam stood outside by Kayla's car watching. When G got into the house, Sam came up to Kayla's car.

Sam: What the fuck is going on?
Kayla: Your guess is as good as mine.
Sam: I don't believe this nigga is doing this shit.
Kayla: I can't believe he disrespected me again.

G came rushing out the house, fussing and cussing. Kayla got out of the car, arguing with him. G came up to Kayla, and they started fighting. He hit her in the face, busting her lip.

Kayla, repeating: Oh, you gonna hit me?
G: You hit me in my motherfucking head, bitch.
Kayla: So what, bitch!

They kept fighting. Sam grabbed G and got him from fighting Kayla.

G: Get you hands off me.
Trick: G, just come in the house.
G: You shut the fuck up, bitch.

Kayla, holding her lip and crying, made her way to the car. G was still arguing with her and trying to go hit her again. She sat there, and he threatened to get a gun and shoot her. Kayla figured it was time to go. Kayla turned on the interior lights and saw a big hole. Knowing she needed stitches, she went to the hospital.

Chapter Eight

When she got home, she still couldn't believe what went on. She took the medicine the doctor prescribed to her and went to sleep. When she woke up, she saw that she had a call from Evelyn. She called her and told her what happened.

Evelyn: Oh, hell naw. So what you wanna do? Because you know dogg and his crew don't have a problem handling shit.

Kayla: No, he'll get his, and I don't even have to do nothing.

Evelyn: Did he call you?

Kayla: No, and I'm not calling him.

Evelyn: One of y'all gonna call watch.

Kayla: I don't know, but I know my lip is killing me.

Evelyn: Girl, I can't believe how disrespectful he is. And then he gonna bring a bitch to your car. Shit, I would have did more than hit him in the head.

Kayla: Girl, I was holding back.

Evelyn: Why?

Kayla: Call me stupid, but I let my guard down and started loving him.

Evelyn: I knew it. I was just waiting for you to say it. You know not to fall in love with a youngster. They not ready. They still in puberty, girl, you know that.

Kayla: I know. I wish I would have never met him.

Evelyn:　You know, it's gonna be hard to let him go, right?
Kayla:　Yeah, but I have to. I just don't know what led to it.
Evelyn:　To what?
Kayla:　All the arguing and fighting.
Evelyn:　Well, I don't know who started after I left, but you started the one in the driveway.

Evelyn went on telling Kayla what happened with the first fight. Kayla didn't know that she started it. It made her feel bad and guilty. Then she started thinking if she didn't start that one, maybe the other one wouldn't have happened. After she got off the phone with Evelyn, she called G. He didn't answer, so she left a voice mail, apologizing for last night's first fight. As the days went on without hearing from G, she started missing him. Tony was calling her, and she wouldn't answer the phone. She got up and sat at the computer to get on Facebook. Since she knew that he gets on Facebook, she decided to put a status up that she thought would make him mad. It said, "If a nigga can't respect you, just bust his ass in the back of his head! You know who you are." And needless to say that there were a lot of people who agreed with her and commented. Right after that, she got a call from Evelyn.

Kayla:　Hello.
Evelyn:　Guess what?
Kayla:　What?
Evelyn:　You know that bitch, Trick?
Kayla:　Yeah.
Evelyn:　Well, she's a stripper.
Kayla:　Are you serious?
Evelyn:　Yes, and that's not the worst of it. She is fucking around with two of G's boys.
Kayla:　Hell no. But that's the woman that he loves though. Wow! How did you find out? Sam? Did G find out?
Evelyn:　No, Sam didn't tell me. I did a little investigating of my own, and no, G don't know because it's still happening.

They both laughed.

Evelyn: So are you gonna tell him, or will I have the pleasure?
Kayla: No, let him find out on his own. I tell you, revenge is a motherfucker. That's what he gets with his punk ass. I wonder what's gonna happen when he do find out.

They continued to talk. Then Tony clicked in on the other end. Weeks went by after the incident with Kayla and G. Kayla was on a date with Tony. He was telling her about how his daughter was in an abusive relationship. They got deep into the conversation, so deep that Kayla forgot that she was talking with Tony. She started going on about how she and G got into it recently.

Tony: So this happened recently.

Kayla looked surprised and was speechless.

Tony: Kayla?
Kayla: Yeah.
Tony: So you lied to me, and on top of that, this nigga bust your lip, and you couldn't tell me?
Kayla: Tony, I didn't tell you be—
Tony, cutting her off: I was concerned about you, and you lied to me. I told you I was married because I didn't want to lie to you or keep secrets from you.

He called for the waiter to pay the bill. On the way home, they didn't talk at all. When he pulled up to Kayla's house, Kayla apologized.

Tony: I accept your apology, but you lost my trust, and because of that, I can't see you anymore.
Kayla: Look, I never intended to hurt you, and I never lied to you about anything. I just didn't tell you. I didn't know

how you would react. Besides, you're married, and I didn't have a problem with that.

Tony: First of all Kayla, I'm a grown man. I know how to react to certain situations. Second, I told you I was married, but you didn't tell me that you were seeing someone.

Kayla: It's not like that. It's just a fling.

Tony: Whatever it is, enjoy.

Kayla: I'm sorry.

Tony: Me too.

Kayla looked at Tony with her eyes full of tears and turned to get out of the car. Even though Tony was upset, mad, and hurt, he was still a gentleman and waited for Kayla to get into the house before he pulled off. Kayla went into her room and threw her stuff on the bed and sat down. "What the hell did I do?" She started calling herself dumb and stupid for even bringing it up. She picked up the phone to call Evelyn.

Evelyn: Hey, girl.

Kayla: Hey. Tony found out about me and G getting into it.

Evelyn: You told him?

Kayla: Yeah, by mistake though.

Evelyn: How by mistake?

Kayla: We was talking about abusive relationships, and I thought I was talking to someone else, and it just came out.

Evelyn: Girl, that's some bullshit.

Kayla: What?

Evelyn: I think you wanted him to know.

Kayla: No, I really didn't.

Evelyn: Well, now what you gonna do? You fucked up with Tony, and you and G not talking. I guess we got to go club hopping again.

They both laughed.

Evelyn: Let me ask you a question.

Kayla: Shoot.

Evelyn: Did you love, G?

Kayla, with a soft voice: Yeah, I did.

Evelyn: Now that was your mistake. It was supposed to be a fling thing. You weren't supposed to let it happen. In this situation, you're the adult. You were supposed to have control, not him. He's just a baby. You can't fall in love with a man living the single life. You know why? Because he's saying he's gonna be a hoe, girl.

Kayla started laughing

Evelyn: And you know what else?

Kayla: What?

Evelyn: That pregnant bitch that came over to your house with, G? Well, I heard she wanted to keep the baby, and he beat her ass so bad that she had a miscarriage. That nigga has a temper, and something is gonna happen to him, so you're making the right choice by leaving him alone.

Kayla held the phone quietly, feeling sorry for the girl, but she was more concerned about her situation. No matter what she did, she couldn't stop thinking about the good times she and G had. After her friend told her how she really started the fight, she thought it would be only right to apologize, even though she already did. But she decided to write a letter. She found enough courage to send it off two days later.

A couple of weeks after that, while Kayla and Evelyn were at the mall, Kayla received a text from G, but it didn't say anything. They kept shopping. Once they finished, they went to the car. While she was driving, she received another text from G that said, "Would you like to stop by and talk?" Kayla looked at it over and over. She took a deep breath and sighed.

Evelyn: What you gonna do?

Kayla: I don't know.

Evelyn: Well, you know what I think, but this is your life, and
          whatever you decide, I'm with you because you're my girl.
Kayla: Thanks, girl.
Evelyn: I just don't want to see you hurt.
Kayla: I could just go and talk to him and nothing else.
Evelyn: Okay, you want me to go with you?
Kayla: No, I'll be okay, but I got your number on speed dial.
Evelyn: Because you know I'll come and bring the dogs. Don't play.

They both laughed. Kayla dropped Evelyn off, but before she
got out, they gave each other a hug.

Evelyn: Be careful and call me when you finish.
Kayla: Okay. Love you.
Evelyn: Love you too.

While Kayla sat there, she sent a text to G. "How do I know
you won't try anything?"

He replied, "Girl, bye, it's up to you."

Kayla thought it would be safe, so she headed over there. When
she got there, she parked, cut the car off, and blew the horn. He
came out and opened the door.

G: Are you coming in?
Kayla: No, I think it would be best if we stay out here.
G: Okay, I'll be back.

He went back in the house and came out with drinks. He got
in the car.

G: How you been?
Kayla: Good. You?
G: All right. I got your letter today.
Kayla: Oh well, I figured I'd apologize that way again.
G: Again?
Kayla: Yeah, I had left a voice message on your phone.

G: Oh, I don't even check my messages.
Kayla: Oh.

There was a moment of silence for a while. Kayla thought to herself, *Is this nigga gonna apologize or what?*

G: You know, I really didn't mean to disrespect you like that. I needed some money from her, and the only way she would give it to me is if I did what I did, and I'm sorry for that. You deserve better. I apologize. You know, I actually missed you.

Kayla did not know if he's telling the truth or lying. He's so good with lying with a straight face to get what he wants.

Kayla: Mmm… well, I missed you too. To be honest, all I could think about was you. I even told Tony about you.
G: You did? Why?
Kayla: Well, actually, it was a mistake. I was talking about you, and it's like I was talking to Evelyn or someone else, and it just came out.
G: So what now?
Kayla: He don't want to see me anymore.
G: Wow. So do you forgive me?
Kayla: Yeah, even though I had to get three stitches.
G: Oh, pooh, let me see. Are you okay now?
Kayla: Yeah, I'm fine.

He kissed her lip. His daughter came out and told him about the chicken burning.

Maria: Hi, Ms. Kay.
Kayla: Hi, Maria. How are you?
Maria: Fine.
Kayla: That's good. She's so cute.

G: Yeah, well, me and my daughter were in there cooking chicken. Do you think you can come back after I feed her and put her to bed?

Evelyn: Me and Evelyn were going out anyway, so I probably could stop by after.

G: Okay, call me and let me know.

Kayla: Okay.

Kayla drove off. She pulled up in front of Evelyn's house and blew the horn. Evelyn came out sharp as hell and got in the car.

Evelyn: Well?

Kayla: Well what?

Evelyn: How did it go?

Kayla: It went well. We talked, he apologized, and he asked me if I could come back after he and his daughter finished cooking chicken and he put her to bed.

Evelyn: You met his daughter?

Kayla: Yeah, well, I have met her.

Evelyn: Oh well, maybe he's growing up after all, letting you meet his daughter and all. So, horny, are you going back?

Kayla: Yeah, I think so.

Evelyn: Well, anyway, what club we going to?

Kayla: I don't know. Any idea?

Evelyn: Let's go to the sugar daddy club. You need to find one to replace the one you had. You just messed it up for the both of us.

Kayla: Girl, you crazy.

They went to the club and got in. Kayla wore a black off-shoulder shirt, gray silky skirt, and sandals, and her hair and nails and toes were done to perfection. She knew she looks good. A lot of men asked her to dance, but only a few got the opportunity. As she and Evelyn sat there with drinks that men had bought them, she saw Tony with another woman. He saw her, and they looked at each other eye to eye, and he suddenly turned away. It hurt her to see him with another woman, but they were bound to break up anyway. As it got late, they decided they were ready to go. Right then, G called.

Kayla: Hey.
G: Hey, pooh, are you still coming?
Kayla: Yeah, I was getting ready to leave out now.
G: Okay.

Kayla was driving Evelyn home.

Kayla: So do you think I should wear this or should I change?
Evelyn: Well, if you plan on fucking, which I know you are, there's nothing like easy access.

They looked at each other and said, "A dress with no panties!" They both laughed. They talked all the way to Evelyn's house. When they arrived, Evelyn got out of the car and went in.

Chapter Nine

On the way to G's house, there was a traffic accident on the freeway, so it was taking her a while to get there. G called.

Kayla: Hello.

G: Where you at, pooh?

Kayla: On the freeway. There's an accident, but I'm about to come up and find another route.

G: Okay, well, I wanted to go to the store, but by the time I get there, they'll be closed, so can you pick up some Svedka, cranberry juice, and a can of beer, and I'll give you the money when you get here?

Kayla: Yeah, I'll get it.

Kayla finally made it over to G's house. She blew the horn, and out came G. He got in the car, smelling good and looking good. Kayla stared at him like she just wanted to jump on him. He leaned over and gave her a kiss. They heard the house door close. They looked, and here came Sam up to the car.

Sam: Hey, Kayla, nice to see you again.

Kayla: Hey, Sam, same here.

Sam: I thought that was the end of y'all. Y'all was tripping that night. Where y'all going?

G, looking at Kayla: We don't know yet. I was thinking about the drive-in since that's the only thing that's open, if it's okay with you.

Kayla: That'll be fun.

Sam: Well, on the way, can y'all drop me over my girl's house?

Kayla: Yeah, I don't mind.

Sam went and closed the house door.

G: Pooh, why don't you let Sam drive and sit in the back with me?

Kayla: Can he drive?

G, laughing: Yeah, bay.

Sam came out and got ready to get in the car.

Kayla: Sam, can you drive?

Sam: What? Don't I work on cars too?

Kayla: Oh, I'm sorry.

Sam: Yeah, I'll drive.

Sam got in the driver seat, and Kayla got all the way in the back with G. Sam got the radio playing while he's driving, and Kayla and G were in the back, talking and drinking.

G: Let me eat that pussy while Sam driving.

Kayla: He'll be able to see us.

G: No, he can't. Just let me taste it.

Kayla: Not with him in the car.

G: Okay.

They got to Sam's girl's house. He told them to hold on to make sure she's there, and she was. Sam came back to the car and asked them if they could pick him back up.

G: How long you gonna be?

Sam: Not long.

G, looking at Kayla: Well, we might as well not go and just wait here in the car for him.

Kayla: Okay.

Sam went back on the porch with his girl. G reached over and started kissing Kayla. Kayla kissed him in return. He went and put on a Brandy song, "Have You Ever," and went in the back. They started kissing again, and Kayla started rubbing his dick hard and fast.

G: Damn, pooh, you been wanting this, huh?

Kayla: For the longest, nigga. You just don't know.

They kissed even more. G then got on his knees and opened Kayla's legs. He saw that she didn't have panties on.

G: Damn, and you ready and wet.

Kayla: Yeah, because of you.

G moaned and went in for the kill. Faster and faster, he's licking her clit. Kayla's moving her ass up and down fast. Getting ready to cum, she lifted her ass, and G's moving right with her. A loud moan came from Kayla as she grabbed the back of the seat. G hurried and put his dick in her pussy before she could finish cumming. As soon as he put it in, he moaned.

G: Damn, this shit is good and hot.

Kayla: Fuck it harder.

G: You sure you can handle it?

Kayla: What's my name?

G started fucking her faster and harder. Kayla was enjoying every bit of the pleasurable pain he was giving her. Kayla told him to get up and sit on the seat. She climbed on him and started riding. Grabbing her ass, he moaned loud and squeezed her ass hard. He's getting ready to cum but didn't want Kayla to stop. All of a sudden, with a loud grunt, he released. Kayla got up. Both of them running with sweat, they went to the front and turned the radio down. G started the car up and started driving.

Kayla: Where you going?
G: Just driving around because it's hot.

They started talking and laughing about what just happened. Kayla, looking at G and still horny, leaned over and unzipped his pants and started sucking his dick while he's driving. G pulled over and pulled his pants down so that Kayla could reach it better and started back driving. Kayla kept sucking until he busted his nut. Even though G was swerving and moaning, Kayla still kept sucking and swallowing until every drop was gone. G drove back to the house where Sam was at and parked. Leaning back, hot and tired, G told Kayla to get her ass in the back.

Kayla: Huh?
G: Get that ass in the back. I want some more of that.
Kayla: We just did it.

G looked at her quietly and boo-boo faced, not saying a word. Kayla could tell something was wrong.

Kayla: What's wrong? You want me to get this ass in the back?
G: Yes, get that ass in the back.

Kayla got up smiling, going to the back of the car with G right behind her. He went down and ate the pussy again. And once again, Kayla came quickly. He told her he wanted her to get on her knees. Kayla got on knees and bent her back all the way down.

G, rubbing his hands on it: Damn, look at this ass.

He started banging her pussy from the back real hard. Kayla's going crazy, grabbing the seat belts and biting on them, taking her hand and putting it behind her, trying to push him off. He fucked even harder. They both released at the same time. Breathing hard and fast, G opened all the doors to the car.

G: Smell nothing but pussy in her.
Kayla: You did it, nigga.

They both laughed and were hungry. While they were waiting for Sam, they decided to go get something to eat. They went to the Coney Island. While they were waiting for the food, Kayla saw a girl looking at G. Kayla, still drunk, was going to say something to the girl, but G grabbed her.

G: Pooh, don't start.
Kayla, loud: I see y'all giving each other the starry eyes and shit.
G: Pooh, don't start, please.

They got their food and headed back to Sam. Sam came to the car.

Sam: Y'all didn't get me nothing?
G: Nigga, you just got through eating your mixed chicken.

They all started laughing because Sam's girl is mixed.

G, giving him two wingdings: Here, nigga.
Sam: Naw, man, I don't want none. Y'all about ready?
G: We waiting on you.
Sam: I'm ready.

Sam got in the car. G drove back to his house. Sam got out, but G and Kayla stayed in the car and finished eating. Once they got finished, they said their good-byes and ended the night or morning with a kiss.

G: Call me when you get home.
Kayla: Okay.

Chapter Ten

The next day, Evelyn and Kayla had planned to go to the movies. But because Kayla was tired from earlier, she wanted to cancel, but she didn't. It was time to go. On her way to get Evelyn, she got a call from G.

Kayla: Hello.
G: I need you over here now.
Kayla: What's wrong?
G: I need you to come over here.
Kayla: I was—
G, cutting her off: Look, pooh, I need you over here now, please.
Kayla: Okay, G, okay.

Kayla called Evelyn and told her that something came up over G's house, and she'll be there when she finds out what's wrong and make sure everything is okay. Speeding to get there, she hoped that nothing bad happened to G. She pulled up and parked in front of G's house. She got ready to get out, but G's storming out the house. He came on the driver side and told her to slide over. He's driving. Kayla slid over in the passenger seat. G got in and slammed the door. He started up the car, turned the radio up, and started driving. Kayla was wondering what's wrong and why was he acting like that.

Kayla, turning the radio down: What's wrong?

G didn't say anything and turned the radio back up. Kayla repeated the same thing as did G. Kayla did it again.

Kayla: What's wrong?
G, turning it back up: Please don't touch the radio again.

They drove in silence. He stopped at a store to get some drinks. He got back in the car, still not talking, just the music playing from the radio. Kayla's looking at G, wondering what was going through his mind and what he could be upset about. Looking at him thinking how sexy he looks when he's angry, she came back to reality, knowing something isn't right. He turned into a motel room. After paying for the room, he parked her car in front of the door. They got out of the car, and G slammed the door, making Kayla jump. He went and opened the room door for them to go in. Kayla sat in the chair, while G put the drinks on the table. Too scared to sit too close to him, she got up and sat on the bed. Shortly, G brought her a drink.

Kayla: No, thanks. I don't want any.
G: Drink with me.
Kayla: I don't want to drink, G.
G, with a straight face: Drink with me please.

Kayla grabbed the cup and drank it quickly. G filled her cup up again and sat at the table.

G: Come sit over here by me, please.

Kayla got up and moved to the chair she sat in first, drinking her drink quickly again. She placed the empty cup on the table. Once again, G filled it up. She drank that one quickly too.

Kayla, slamming her cup down: Now can you tell me what's wrong?

G filled her cup up again.

Kayla: No, I don't want anymore.
G: Just one more, I promise.
Kayla, drinks quickly: Oh my god. Now!

G sat down in his chair, with his head slightly bowed down, looking straight at Kayla. Not saying anything like he was waiting for something, he just stared at Kayla. Kayla started getting a buzz from drinking.

Kayla: Look, poppy, are you going to tell me what's going on? Because me and—
G, cutting her off: Did you fuck Sam?
Kayla: What?
G: Did you fuck Sam?
Kayla: Why would you ask me something like that?
G: Did you fuck him? Yes or no, answer.
Kayla: Do you think I fucked him, G?
G: Yes or no?
Kayla, looking at him angrily: G, you really need to think about what you're asking me. And it's not like you would care anyway if I did.
G, getting up: Did you or did you not fuck Sam?
Kayla: G…

G slapped her in her face. Kayla sat there holding her face, crying.

G: All I ask was one simple question, and you couldn't even answer it. Let me know that you did fuck him, you hoe.
Kayla: No, okay, no. I didn't fuck Sam. You're wrong for even thinking I would.

G standing there, watching Kayla cry, started feeling bad. Walking over to her, he tried to hug her.

G: Pooh, look, I'm sorry. That nigga told me that y'all fucked last night while I was sleep, and I went crazy because that happened to me before.

Kayla: With who? Trick the stripper? Me and her are two different people, G. I'm not like that. I'm not a hoe.

G grabbed her face, trying to kiss her.

Kayla: No, G, move. I'm about to go.

G: Pooh, don't do that. I got the room for the whole night.

Kayla: Well, call one of your other hoes over here. I'm sure Trick the bitch will come fuck you for the right price. Matter of fact, the one you should be slapping is Trick because she was fucking two of your boys, and she still is.

Kayla grabbed her purse and keys while G was standing there, looking like he already knew about Trick and his boys. She walked out the door and slammed it shut. G opened the door.

G: Pooh, please don't go. I'm sorry. I love you.

Kayla: Stop playing with me, G.

G: No, I really do. No bullshit.

Kayla stopped walking and turned around in shock. G walked up to her.

G: Look, I'm gonna be honest with you. When I first met you, my plan was to use you for your money. But then I got to know you. Kayla, you're a good woman, and I guess I just wasn't used to dealing with one. Then I started liking you a lot because you're real with yours and you always keep it 100 percent. And then when Sam told me that y'all fucked, it hurt my heart. That's when I finally realized that I love you, and if I lose you, I don't know what I would do.

For the first time, Kayla could tell that he meant what he was saying. His eyes were watery like he wanted to cry. She heard the tremble in his voice when he was talking. Kayla took his hand and kissed him. She led him into the room, and for the first time, Kayla thought they made love instead of straight fucking. There was a difference.

The next morning, G had an interview for a job—a good-paying job seven days a week. The only thing was that the interview was in Ann Arbor, and Kayla already agreed to take him. They woke up early enough to get him there before his scheduled time. Kayla wished him good luck before he got out of the car. Kayla waited for him in the car. When he came out, he had a smile as big as life on his face, so Kayla knew he got the job. He got in the car.

G: I got it! But the job is in Taylor.
Kayla: Congratulations. You'll make it there.
G: We gonna be straight now.
Kayla: Who?
G: Me and you.

Kayla gave him a kiss. On their way home, they stopped at other places on the way to G's house. When they got to G's house, he grabbed his papers and got out of the car. Kayla got out, and G gave her a big hug and a kiss.

G: Thank you for being there for me, pooh.
Kayla: You're welcome. That's how I am.

They both smiled.

G: Are you coming over tonight?
Kayla: You need to be well rested for work tomorrow. Go in there and take a nice shower and relax.

G: Okay, but I'll see you tomorrow, right?
Kayla: Maybe if you're not too tired.
G: Okay, thanks again, baby.
Kayla: Okay.

Kayla went home and told Evelyn the good news. She's telling her all the plans she got set up for her and G and how he told her that he loved her, even about Sam saying that he and her fucked. She gave all details of everything that happened. At 8:00 p.m., Kayla called G.

G: Hey, pooh.
Kayla: Hey, I just wanted to say good night and I'm proud of you.
G: Good night, baby, and thank you.
Kayla: Do you remember when you told me you loved me?
G: Yeah.
Kayla: I love you too, and I been loving you since. I just didn't tell you.
G: I already knew.
Kayla: You did? How?
G: Your actions.
Kayla: Oh okay.
G, laughing: Oh, I'm observant.
Kayla, laughing: Okay, I'm glad I know now. Okay, good night.
G: Good night.

Kayla hung up the phone and lay in bed, smiling until she fell asleep. At 5:30 a.m., the phone rang. It was G.

Kayla, with a sleepy voice: Hello.
G: Hey, baby, I didn't mean to wake you up, but I need a ride to work.
Kayla: Okay, I'm on my way.

Kayla speed drove there so that he won't be late on his first day. When they get to his job, he still had thirty minutes.

G: Damn, pooh, you made sure I wasn't late.

Kayla: Punctuality is very important, especially with a job making what you are.

G: Yeah, true that.

They sat there and talked until ten minutes to seven. It was time for him to go in. Before he got out of the car, he kissed Kayla and told her he'll call her at break, and he did.

Kayla: Hey, baby, how's it going?

G: Baby, this job is so easy. I'll be here for a while.

Kayla: That's good. I got some good news too.

G: What?

Kayla: I got an interview at that new factory they're building.

G: That's what's up, so we both will be getting paid.

Kayla: Yep.

G: Okay, pooh, let me get back in here.

Kayla: Okay, do you need me to pick you up?

G: I'll call and let you know. It's a guy that stay over there by me, and he said I can catch a ride with him, so I might do that and save you some gas.

Kayla: It don't matter, but okay.

Six o'clock came and she still didn't hear from him. She didn't want to call him because she didn't know if he was still working or not. It was way after 7:00 p.m., and she didn't want to call because she thought he might be tired. She didn't hear from him for a whole week. She really didn't worry at that time because she knew that he had to get back used to getting up and working again. She didn't say anything to Evelyn because she didn't want to hear anything negative. It's now Sunday night, and Kayla's phone rang. It's G.

Kayla: Hello.

G: Hey, baby.

Kayla: Long time no hear.

G: I know. It's just I been so tired. I gotta get used to it.
Kayla: I know.
G: You want to come over and see me?
Kayla: You sure you're not too tired?
G: No, I want to see you.
Kayla: Okay, I'll be there in a minute.

Kayla hung up the phone and got dressed and headed over to G's house. On the way, she stopped at the store and brought him a celebratory drink. When she pulled up, she saw that he's on the porch. He got in the car.

G, kissing her: Hey, baby.
Kayla: Hey, here you go.
G: Aw, baby, you didn't have to do that.
Kayla: You deserve it.
G: Thanks, baby. I sure can use it. We could go in the house, but it's junky and noisy, all them niggas in there.
Kayla: Well, we can stay in here. It don't matter.

They sat in the car and talked for a while. Kayla saw that it was 11:30 p.m., and being concerned about him resting, she told him she was about to go.

G: Okay, pooh, I'll talk to you tomorrow, but call me when you get home so I'll know you made it.
Kayla: Okay, love you.
G: Love you too, baby.
Kayla: Will you need a ride to work?
G: No, my mom gonna let me use her car.
Kayla: Okay.

Kayla went home and called G. He talked to her for a little while. He was talking about how he was gonna take her out to eat, to the movies, to the bar, and to everything. He had all kinds of plans. Well, guess what? He lied. She never heard from him for a long, long time. He used her time and her gas to make sure he got a job to take care of another bitch. That same bitch could have taken him to get the job. She felt betrayed, hurt, heartbroken, and stabbed in the back. To this day, she can't understand why he did it. She still hears from him every now and then, but it's not like she wants to.

So to all of my older ladies who are dating younger men or are thinking about it, don't be like Kayla. You might get lucky and find one that's real, but for the ones that are not, don't spend your hard-earned money on no young nigga. Kayla went out of her way for this young nigga, and he played her all that time, even when he told her he loved her. He should have won a Grammy because that was a good act. I don't care how good the dick is, how good he ate the pussy, how good he looks, or how good he smells. Don't give up the loot. Kayla learned her lesson for real. If he needed your money, then he's not worth it. And G really wasn't.

Printed in the United States
By Bookmasters